D.W.
The Big Boss

by Marc Brown

LITTLE, BROWN AND COMPANY

New York ᨋ Boston

D.W. was feeling bossy. Even bossier than usual!

Her father was making a cake.

"It needs more sugar," she told her father.
"I'm pretty sure this is the right amount," said Dad.
"More sugar," D.W. insisted. "Or it will taste yucky."

Mom was in her office, working.
"It's messy in here," D.W. declared.
"That's okay," said Mom. "I know where everything is."

"Messy, messy, messy," said D.W. "You really need to clean up this place."

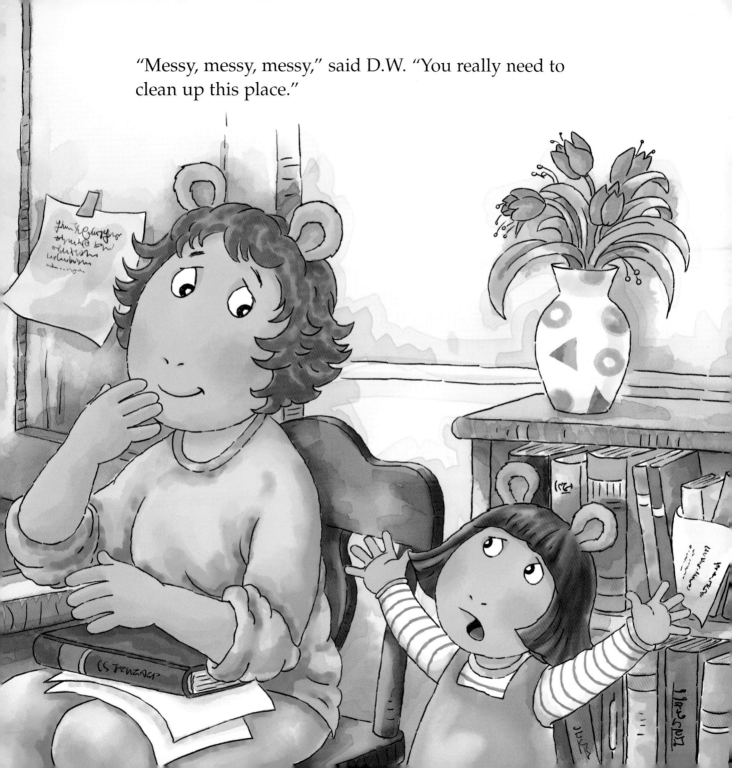

"You're saying it all wrong," D.W. said to Kate.
Kate's eyes opened wide.
"It's *goo goo gaa gaa*," D.W. explained. "Not *gaa gaa goo goo*."

At bedtime, she stopped Arthur in the middle of a story. "Your voices all sound the same," she complained. "I'm doing the best I can," said Arthur.

"Well," sniffed D.W., "you really need to practice."

"What's for breakfast?" D.W. asked the next morning.
"Nothing, I'm afraid," Dad told her.
"But I'm hungry!" said D.W. "And you *always* cook me breakfast."

"Sorry," said Dad. "I'm afraid I'll do it wrong."

D.W. rushed into Mom's office.
"You're not dressed!" said D.W. "We're going to be late for my play date!"

Mom shrugged. "I can't worry about that. I have to figure out how to clean up my office."

"Mom and Dad are acting weird," D.W. said to Arthur.
"We need to do something."

Arthur pointed to his throat. "Can't talk," he whispered.
"Might use the wrong voice."

"This family needs more help than I thought," D.W. said to herself. "I'd better do something—fast."

She went back to the kitchen. "You make the best meals in the whole world, Dad. Could you please try again?"
He nodded. "I'll see what I can do."

While she was waiting, D.W. went into Mom's office.
"I could help you clean up the mess, Mom. Then you could get dressed."
Mom smiled. "Thank you, D.W."

D.W. found Arthur playing with Kate. "When your voice feels better,"
she said nicely, "maybe you could read me another story."
Arthur cleared his throat. "It does feel a little better."

Kate looked up at D.W.

D.W. folded her arms. "It's still *goo goo gaa gaa*," she said.

"But I know you'll get it right soon!"